Winnie G
The Witches

This page may be blank, but you my fellow witches are far from blank.

To forge your own destiny, you will use your imagination and believe in yourself.

Happy Witch crafting...

Winnie G
The Witches

This story includes as a bonus your own Book of Shadows.

Jean Megaw

Published By:

ThreeZombieDogs®

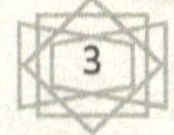

This book is a work of fiction, Names, characters etc. are either a product of the author's imagination or are used fictitiously. Any resemblance to actual persons, living, dead or still to be born 'may or may not' be entirely coincidental.

Any reality is to demonstrate a real, current, and debatable feel to the story. All characters names in this book can be personalised by the publisher to create your own personal storybook.

No part of this book can be reproduced in any form, including but not limited to; written, electronic or mechanical, including photocopying, recording, or by any information retrieval system without the written permission from the publishing company.

The right of Jean Megaw to be identified as author of this work has been asserted by her in accordance with Copyright, Designs, and Patents Act, 1988

Although every precaution has been taken in the preparation of this book, the publisher and author assume no responsibility for errors or omissions. Neither is any liability assumed for damages resulting from the use of information contained herein.

Published by Three Zombie Dogs® McLaughlin's Close, Derry, BT48 6SZ. All rights reserved. Copyright © 2017 Jean Megaw

A copy of this book has been deposited at The Legal Deposit Office, The British Library. ISBN: 9781912039654 First Published Nov 2017.

For

My family, past, present and future.

And

Every child throughout
The universe.

Without earth's children... well... there
would be 'No one Here!'

Thanks, Eve!

Personalise This Book

https://www.jeanmegaw.com

Personalise this book, by getting the names of the cast changed to your own choice of names. See website for a list of the names that can be changed.

Bonus: Photo to Sketch

In the Bonus 'Book of Shadows', we will turn your photograph into a black & white Sketch drawing.

Rocky Lizard
YouTuber

https://www.youtube.com/c/rockylizard

Subscribe to his channel to watch some cool kids' videos.

Winnie 'G' - The Witches

By Jean Megaw

Bonus:

This book contains your personal copy of the

'Book of Shadows'

Winnie G, gives you 2 starter spells, 1 bonus spell and enough pages for 13 of your own spells. Have fun creating your own magic spells.

Some Witch Facts:

- A Witch can be female or male
- Wichelen = To bewitch or forecast
- Wiccan = Pagan Witchcraft
- Witchcraft = Practice of Magic, either alone or in a group (coven)
- There are Good Witches, Winnie G
- There are Bad Witches, Winnie B
- There are White, Black, Red, Blue and Green magic
- Then there is the witchcraft of Winnie G. This is witchcraft for the young. Aha ha ha ha

Inspirational Thoughts

Write down some of your thoughts on the subjects below. Your thoughts create your magical beginning and bring you to the infinite universe as one and as a Witch.

Past:

Present:

Future:

Author memories

My best bedtimes were stories being read to me as I lay in bed or on the sofa unless of course, I was tormenting my sister and brothers.

These stories came directly from the improvisation of a responsible adult. A responsible adult who terrified us little ones, with actions that made it seem real. Scenes in movies include dramatic music that chills our bones and sets the horror scene in motion. Who needed music when you had Aunt Jean's actions?

Every night that she was with us, we listened to her endless Good Winnie and Bad Winnie the witch stories, enthralled in her every word. And when she was not in our house, our mum and dad had to stand in...But Aunts Jean's were always the best. That was over fifty years ago. Since then I have told these stories to my own children and to my nephews and nieces as they all grew up.

Jean Megaw

"Please Aunt Jean, just one more story?"

Dedicated to our Aunt Jean

The good witch

Winnie G - The Witches

Once upon a time...

... There was a Good Witch and a Bad Witch. They had only two things in common. First, they were both witches and second they had the same name, "Winnie."

They lived in different parts of the country in their own separate cottages. One cottage was nice and uplifting, the other was dirty, stinky and smelled of magic potion that was seriously rotten.

One Witch was good and the other, well let's say very naughty. How naughty did I hear you ask? So naughty that there was not a 'naughty chair' big enough to sit her naughty bum on!

Bad Winnie the witch was not always bad, she started off life as a good witch. Both Winnie's were best of friends at one time. Then one day, she got jealous of good Winnie the witches new partner. He too was a Witch, he and good Winnie met at the autumn witchcraft ball. That first moment when their eyes caught a glimpse of each other, shooting stars lit up the night sky. And since then they became bonded together in a union of love.

Bad Winnie the witch soon became angry and resentful. She was no longer the sole subject of good

Winnie's life. Despite Good Winnie's attempts at trying to preserve her friendship, the bad witch went on her own pathway. She turned away from white magic and jumped straight into a cauldron of black magic.

Good Winnie was so upset about losing her friend to bad magic, that she often cried herself to sleep. Her partner Ailig decided that he would visit Bad Winnie and attempt to bring her back to their white magic circle. Ailig thought his witchcraft powers were strong enough to beat her black magic spells.

Convincing Bad Winnie was not as easy as he thought and Ailig tried his hardest to convince Bad Winnie, but even his spells were no good. As he turned away to leave the cottage, Bad Winnie cast a black magic spell on Ailig, and he became lost to good Winnie the Witch forever.

Good Winnie still tries to this day to find a spell to break bad Winnie's curse. And she will continue to do so until her 'Ailig' returns to be by her side.

While Good Winnie looks for many ways to try and reverse the evil spell, she still has a job to be done.

Anyways, enough about the past, it's the future you have to be careful about. Why? Because bad Winnie loves discovering new ways to remove children from their homes. She usually pries on children fighting, unhappy kids or better still those that sit all on their own. So the next time you see a kid on their own, go ask them to play!

Safety from the bad Witch is in numbers:

One child and all alone? She can snatch you in a flash
Two children fighting, she can whisk you away in a dash

Three or more kids, for the bad witch it becomes a tougher clash

Remember! All alone or fighting? This is a good distraction for her devious skills.

The bad witch would spin tales and catch the children unaware. She would SNATCH them up and WHISK the children back to her home and work them till they fell asleep with exhaustion.

She would make her captured children scrub the floors on their hands and knees until you could see the blood seep from the scabs on their knees. She would make you clean her yard with a brush missing half its hairs, and the yard had to be spotless! And then to top it all off, she would make you cook rabbit and cockroach stew. Cooked in an old black rusty cauldron, perched over a fire made from sticks, and bones from god know's what?

While the children stirred her dinner, the witch would throw magic dust into the pot. She cast spells from **her Black Magic Book of Shadows**, that's her magic book full of evil magic spells. The pages were made from the skin of captured children that did not escape, or so we were told. The cover of this book... well, I dare not tell you, for you would never leave your bedroom... unless she dragged you out from beneath the covers with her long sharp fingernails. They were so long that they would scratch the ground as she walked making a terrifying screeching sound that ran shivers up and down your spine.

We once heard tales of her magic dust turning the stew in the cauldron into a fiery beast. It would glare at you with its bright, frightful, and large rounded red eyes. Then the beast would cough flames that burnt you to a crisp, and finally, he would devour your burnt body.

By removing every trace of your existence including your toys and clothes, the beast had ensured that you never EVER existed on earth.

Log 1: The Missing Children & Bad Winnie the Witch

It was a hot summer's day, and I was out playing in our front garden with my brother Jim, my sister Jean and our two dogs, Chippy and Lassie. My sister and brother started disagreeing and fighting over who is to get MY ball. Chippy and lassie were barking at each other, they too were fighting for MY Greenock Morton ball.

I sprinted into the house. "Aunt Jean, they are ALL fighting over my ball again, and I want it back, RIGHT NOW!"

"Ok, Rik lets sort it out. "Have all the midges gone? You know they eat me alive? "And I am not going out there if..." Rik interrupted his Aunt.

"Of course, there are no midges, I lit a fire with all the wet twigs I gathered up from underneath our tree house, and the wet wood creates lots of smoke and that keeps them midges away."

They both go out to the garden, but the garden is empty of children and the ball...

["Stop your fighting little children, I need your help. " Will you help this wee frail old woman, Oh Please?"

Jim said, "I'm in the scouts, I will do my good deed for the day!"

"I'm in the girl guides, I will do my good deed as well. What would you like us to do for you, mam?"

The old ladies hood was covering her face as she spoke. "Come closer and look at my walking stick, I think it got broken. I tripped and fell over your tortoise. What's it doing out here on the street?" Jean and Jim rushed over as fast as they could. They asked the old lady, "Is Tina our tortoise alright?" said as they took one step out of the garden, and with one fell swoop, the old lady grabbed them by the arm. Her hood fell down and they screamed for help, "It's bad..."

But it was too late,

They have been snatched away from the gate, chippy and lassie barked and tore with their teeth at the witches' cloak, but she kicked them to the ground and they fell with a whimper.

The ball fell from Jeans grip...]

...bounced less and less until it became motionless on the ground.

Aunt Jean screamed, "Where are Jean and Jim?" As Rik picks up the ball he shouts "look," pointing to Chippy and Lassie. "Is that a piece of broomstick in their mouths?" The dogs ran over together wagging their tails while holding the stick in both their mouths, neither were

letting the other have the stick on

their own.

"Oh No! Bad Winnie the witch has snatched my children." Auntie fell to the ground crying. I wrapped my arms around her shoulders, pulling her towards me and said with a firm voice "That's my brother and sister, I will sing the magic song and Good Winnie the Witch will help us. Don't you worry, I will have them home before mum and dad gets back."

The magic song:

'Good Winnie the witch, Good Winnie,
I sing your name,

We are all one of the same,

Come quickly, quicker than the Magic dust,

In you we trust."

Log 2 Good Winnie the Witch

Within a few seconds, she lands on the grass. Good Winnie climbs off her broomstick and tells Broomie to search for clues. Broomie wags its bristles and begins to brush the grass, looking for any traces that will help find the missing children.

Aunt Jean explains the story while chippy and lassie drops the piece of broomstick at good Winnie the witch's feet for analysis.

"Uhmn...Yes...Yuk... as she shakes the dog's dripping and foaming salvia from the stick...this is definitely a piece of a broomstick and it is from Bad Winnie the Witches Broom." Chippy and lassie both barked as if to agree with Winnie, but I think they just wanted the stick back to play with.

Good Winnie rubbed her hairy chin...chin... then she pulled her White Magic Book of Shadows from her long magic cloak, she cast a spell on the bad broomstick and turned towards me and said, "Let's go get the children back, Aunt Jean, you stay here and take care of the baby."

"Rik, I will need your help. Bad Winnie will not let me near her home. She has a special spell to stop other witches getting close to her forest."

Rik turned to his Auntie, "Don't you worry, Aunt Jean? I will help Good Winnie return them home safely."

Log 3 Magic Broomstick

"Hold tight for take-off!" Good Winnie flew as fast as a cannonball up into the sky.

"How will you know which way to go?" Rik asks with the wind flapping his mouth open and shut. It sounded like bla...bla...bla.

"This piece of broomstick is full of bad magic, watch as I let it go"

Rik, nearly fell off Broomie as he shouted with excitement, "Look, a piece of stick is flying on its own."

"All we have to do is follow the stick. Rik, make sure you keep your eyes on that rag end of a broomstick."

They flew high in the sky, even the seagulls flapped their wings, pointing in the direction that we had to travel.

"I have an idea for your public relations image, what about Winnie G? Its hip, like Honey G on the X-Factor. Honey G 'RAPS, but Winnie G ... Well, I'm working on that!"

"Sounds great Rik, everyone can call me Winnie G, 'G' can be short for Good. "I love my new name."

The clouds were filled with water and some even drenched us. But no sooner were we wet, than Broomie had us dried with her magic. It sure was a magical broomstick, it kept us warm and fed us food and drink when we got hungry. I even got a Hot Chocolate!

Looking down towards earth, everything appeared so small. Whoosh.... as we overtook an aeroplane. I was waving at everyone, but no one waved back.

Winnie G explained that the magic made us invisible, but not to the birds or any other animal.

"Winnie there are two 'Sticky Back Rappers' waving at us, to stop!" We turned around and flew over. They began to Rap at us.

"Yo! You Witch and little Rik,

That Bad Witch would make you sick

We are the Sticky Back Rappers

Not your ordinary Flappers

Cody and leflia are our names

That broomstick bit

Is full of misdirection

Don't follow, Go north for forty flaps, then west until you see the forest. That will be the best way!"

No sooner had they appeared, they were gone. We followed their direction, "We are nearly there Rik! Hold on tight, we are going to dive!"

We fell from the sky faster than a rocket going to space and faster than I could eat a packet of double chocolate digestive biscuits, yummy.

"Look Winnie G, there's a forest with smoke, it's coming out of the centre. I'm sure that's Winnie B's hiding spot."

Log 4 Cameron the Dragon Lizard

We landed at the edge of the forest, I got off the Broomie and sat on a massive stone. "Winnie G, what's happening?"

The stone was moving and carrying me along with it.

Laughing her words out "That's a dragon lizard, it's giant and magical and they live near a witches homes. The dragons are always good, but this lizard is special."

I fell off and the dragon lizard and rolled in front of him, "He licked my face."

"You're both friends for life, "When a dragon lizard licks you, you are now one, joined together, one of the same"

I licked him back and smiled, the lizard gave a purr like a cat, then a roar like a lion. Strange, I was not scared when he roared, and I understood everything that he said. He told me that when I needed his help to roar his name, 'Cameron', three times and he would come to me.

"Let's go, Rik, we need to travel on foot now. My magical broomstick does not work near another witches home"

The forest was thick, the branches and bushes were closely knit together, and it was difficult to get through. Good Winnie shouted, "It will take us forever."

Log 5 Lion Muncher's

I felt a tap on my shoulder, there were two little Lion Munchers, tapping away at me.

"Rik, listen to the taps, they talk in Morse code"

Excited, I said, "I was in the scouts we learned Morse code, wait... they are asking.

"O…o …w..e…e…n…e..e..d…h…e…l…p.
"Yeh that's what they said, do we need help?"

I buzzed back in Morse code "buzz…buzz…Yes we do, thanks"
"Our names are David and Lee, now, stand back and follow us."

We took two steps backwards, obviously not enough. For a second we had to close our eyes as the munchers, munched so hard and fast, that the splinters bounced off our faces before falling to the ground. The Lion Munchers made a pathway through the forest. We followed as fast as they made the opening.

When we reached the inner layer of the forest the Lion Munchers stopped. "This is as far as we can munch, good luck." Before they flew away they said their magic chant.

"We are the munchers of bushes and trees
We are the munchers for you and me
Little splinters on the ground
Join your bush and trees, you are found"

No sooner had they finished their chant, and all the splinters began to rise up from the ground, floating back to where they came from. The passage behind us closed as quickly as it had been made.

Log 6 Magic Trees

Magic Lion Munchers, I laughed to myself and was glad for all their help.

"How will we get through the inner forest now Winnie G?"

"Rik, I am sorry, this is as far as I can go. You see us witches are not allowed into the inner circle near other witches home unless we are invited. And I'm certainly not invited."

"Don't you worry Winnie G, I can do this. I am not going to let my sister and brother perish at the hands of that Bad Witch, NO WAY."

I thought, how can I get through this inner forest? The trees were so close together that it made it impossible for even a mouse to squeeze past. Pity the Lion Munchers couldn't help. I paced around the edges for a while, but everywhere I went remained the same. The trees were knitted together like an old woolly jumper.

I considered climbing the trees and clambering over the top. No! The trees were tall, straight and had slippery bark. I tried to climb but kept sliding down and my bum hit the ground with a thump!

"I shall NOT fail my sister and brother," I shouted to the trees.

As coldness began to set in my scout's training jogged my memory,

"Be prepared." So I searched for twigs and lit a fire by rubbing two sticks as fast as I could. The twigs at first let off dense smoke and then like magic burst into golden flames.

There was no protection from Broomie anymore. I stared into the white and red flames of the sparkling fire. The wisdom of the dragon lizard entered my mind. I found a long narrow stick, pierced it into my fire until the end was alight.

I walked towards the inner circle of trees, with the fire stick stretching outwards. Several deep and low pitch scary voices made me jump back in fright! "BRAW...BRAW" they shouted.

"Who goes there?" I asked with my hands shaking, the fire stick dropping splinters of fire ashes onto the ground as I trembled in fear.

"Who goes there, you ASK?" Said an angry bunch of voices.

I waved the stick again, and with a deeper voice mimicking their voice. "WHO GOES THERE? I COMMAND YOU!"

"Well if you command us then we must help you, please lay the fire stick in the bucket of water sitting behind you. We don't want to be burned to ashes, well not just yet. Everyone here is young, most of us are only two hundred years old!"

I dipped the stick into the bucket of water until the fire was extinguished. "I am so sorry, I didn't mean to hurt you. I was only trying to find a way through to help my sister and brother. They are trapped in the Bad Witches home. My name is Rik!" I was amazed the trees were actually talking to me. It went silent for a moment. The trees began whispering to each other.

"We have all decided. I'm the eldest of all the Bark trees, my name is Heather I will help you."
"Jim is my name, I'm the eldest of the Fir trees, and I will help you."

"Pleased to meet you, Rik, I'm Aidan the eldest of the Irish Pine, I will help you."

"Julie is my name, I am the eldest of the Scottish Cucumber Tree, and I will help you."

"Peter, they call me a wild banana, I'm the elder of cairns railway trees. I will help you."

"American chestnut, that's what I'm elder of, but you can call me Paula!"

"I'm no longer brittle, soft or week. I'm elder of the Sassafras trees, made tall and strong with all my companions here. My name is Michael, I will help you."

"Jenifer is my name, pleased to meet you, I'm the youngest of the elders, but I have fiery ginger roots that will protect you. I will help you with all my might."

"We are the babies of the trees, only fifty years old. "Our names are Jodie, Sam, Hayley-S, Jack, Jemma, Hayley, Nathan, Ryan and Savana, we will all help protect you too."

There was a crack of lighting from the sky above and then many wee voices echoed, they all repeated.

"We are yet to be born we are your past, present and future, we are the neem trees." Heather the eldest of the trees, put her fingers to her lips and said, "Shush you little 'sparkles in the eyes', we don't want you to be captured."

"But, we want to help to" the little ones cried.

"There will be time enough for that, now please go back, your time will come soon enough." No sooner had she spoken and they disappeared with a flash of lighting.

Heather whispered to me, "When you are ready to return through our wood. You need only shout as loud as you can. Run little Rabbit, RUN, RUN, RUN"

No sooner had she finished talking, the trees started to part and prepared a pathway, just big enough for me to pass. As I walked through the opening trees, they seemed to bow and then closed immediately behind me. With a whish and a snap, branches became intertwined with each other until there was not even enough space for a minuscule mouse to crawl through.

While walking through the dense forest, the trees collectively said, "We are not here to protect the Bad Witch. We are here to keep everyone safe from wandering into the bad witches clutches. While we have many magical powers like breathing in earth's pollutants and then expelling fresh oxygen to save your planet, we cannot stop the bad witch. That is your task."

Log 7 Calista the Flying Sea Horse

I reached the edge of the witches land and could see Winnie B's cottage. "Good Luck" the trees whispered to me. I took my final step out of their protected forest.

I hid behind a bush and watched Jim, he carried sticks from the garden and Jean, water from the well. They struggled to carry their loads into her cottage.

Winnie B was shouting "Hurry up, you are taking too long! Tonight you will not sleep. Tonight you will work and work and WORK! Ahahaha, Ahahaha, Ahahaha", she screamed in her piercing high pitched voice.

I ran over to the house to peer through the window. There was a tug on my trouser leg "I'm here to help you." I looked down and there hovered a tiny flying Wood Horse, the size of a mouse, and it was talking.

"I came through the woods to help your sister and brother, but the Bad Witch captured me. I get fed scraps, and she makes us all clean-up for her. My name is Calista the Flying wood Horse."

"I would love your help Calista, I need all the help that I can muster."

Looking through the dusty old cottage window, we saw Jean and Jim working away. Stoking the fire and washing the mountains of dishes. They were both chained at the ankle, and the long black chain stretched all the way to Winnie B's chair leg. The key to the lock was around the Bad Witch's neck.

"Keep working, I'm going to sleep now, I'm... so... so... very...very tired. "If you two slackers stop working then I will FEED YOU TO MY DOGS."

Jim turned and shouted back "Slacker, Slacker, you're the one that's a slacker, all you do is sit on your fat bum and we do all the work for you."

Jean shouted "That's right, feed us to your dog's! "Then, there will be no one to do your rotten work for you."

Winnie the bad witch laughed, it was a scary chilling to the bone laugh. Her voice stopped in an instant and she looked at them with her big green witchy eyes and said, "YOU THINK SO? "There are hundreds of children I can steal to replace you two. "Now get to work SLACKERS."

No sooner had she finished speaking and she was fast asleep, snoring her big long pointed nose off, with tiny spiders popping down and up from her nostrils with every grunt that she made.

Log 8 – Winnie B's Cottage

I tip-toed over to the cottage window and gently tapped twice to get their attention. They were delighted at seeing me. But how was I going to free them from their shackles?

Calista, my wood horse friend, whispered, "I'm small enough to climb into the keyhole. "I will use my magic to get the key from around her neck."

No sooner said than done, Calista had retrieved the key and was unlocking their shackles. But the key was magic, every time Calista put the key near the keyhole it bends itself away and to the side.

"Ok, then 'little key' do as I command or I will dip you into cats pee," no sooner than she said that sentence, the key literally jumped from Calista's hand and turned the lock by itself and then began hobbling along the floor to the outside door lock.

"Thank you wee key, you have been so helpful if you wish you can come join us and escape the clutches of Winnie B?" Sadly the key was too frightened and it crawled back over to Winnie B.

Jean, Jim and Calista quietly tip-toed out of the bad witch's cottage.

Log 9 The Escape

Everyone whispered to Calista anxiously. "How will we escape the forest?"

Calista replied calmly "We can all sit on the bad witch's magic broomstick. It will listen to every command that I make, I know the magic words and I will use my magic water."

We climbed onto the broomstick and Calista chanted the magic words.

"Broomstick, Broomstick Listen to me,
Fly like you were a bumble bee.
Listen to me, the wee wood Horse
Three times you circle to the right
Three times you dance in the moonlight
Only once do you glance at me
Cause I will sting you like a bee
Broomstick, Broomstick take us home
We don't want to be all alone"

The broomstick took off, hovering like a helicopter, then we went round in a circle, spiralling upwards until we reached the height of the trees.

Holding on tight,
As tight as we could!
Waiting for the speed of light
But in the coldness of this night
We heard a voice that gave us such
a fright

Log 10 Falling from the Sky

We looked at the bad witch's house from the height of the trees and as we did, we spotted a Bad Witch standing near her 'magical well' shouting!

"Broomstick, Broomstick where are you heading?
Broomstick, Broomstick here is your bedding!

Broomstick, Broomstick I command you to stay!
Broomstick, Broomstick drop them from the sky and onto this pile of rotten and stinky hay"

The air around us flashed and sparkled a rainbow of colours and we landed firmly on the stinky hay. Like scarecrows in a field of smelly old cow's dung, we lept to our feet while pulling the straw from our hair. The foul odour rose from our bodies, like wisps of smoke while we stood there to face the wrath of Winnie B the Witch.

Log 11 Help is on its Way

"Ahahaha, Ahahaha" she laughed, "Now I have three to work for me, give me Calista, I'm going to eat her alive, for she betrayed me.

Calista was climbing out of my pocket to fly over to the evil witch. But I held her tight. "You will not touch my friend." Jean and Jim stood in front of me and said: "You will have to go through us first".

I remembered what Cameron the Dragon lizard told me. Not sure if he could help, I gave him the signal, I roared "CAMERON, CAMERON, CAMERON" three times as loud as I could.

Winnie B the Witch looked startled, she grabbed our sleeves and tried to drag us into her cottage. But before she could, a thunder in the sky, a flash of light and there before our eyes were Cameron the Dragon lizard.

"He can fly" I shouted, my friend, can fly"

Cameron dropped a vapour as he descended from the sky, it was wet and smelly, like an old pair of festering socks that had been soaked in cows dung for months on end. Winnie B the Witch fell to the ground and the stench from the potion began working its magic on her, and quicker than a second, and definitely, before you could say 'stinker', she fell fast asleep.

"I can't fly with everyone on my back and she will only be asleep for five more minutes. Get everyone to safety through the forest, I will keep Winnie B from catching you."

"Run little Rabbit, Run! Run! Run!" I shouted out loud. The trees opened fast and gave us a pathway. The trees replied, "Come! Run as fast as you can".

We ran and ran until we reached the edge of the forest.

"I knew you could do it Rik", said Winnie G as she and Broomie jumped up and down with joy.

"I could not have done it without the help of Calista and Cameron"

Log 12 Spell on Us

Calista climbed out of my pocket and said, "Rik, I have to stay here with my brother Cameron. "We were sister and brother, just like you and your family. "Winnie B captured us and made us work for her. "We managed to escape, but the Bad Witch cast a spell, she turned me into a Wood Horse and Cameron into a Dragon lizard. Winnie G was unable to break her evil spell, but she cast her own spell on us and now we have special powers."

Winnie G said, "Don't worry Calista and Cameron, I will find a spell one day that will turn you back to your earthling form."

There was a loud crackling noise, and thunder from the sky. Winnie G shouted, "Everyone quick, get onto my broomstick."

Calista climbed onto Cameron's back and they flew away to safety.

As we reached the top of the trees on Winnie G's broom, we were met by Winnie B hovering around us. "Ahahaha, I have you all now." These wicked words leached from her mouth while casting a spell with her wicked broomstick.

We had the last laugh, as Cameron and Calista flew from behind and knocked her straight off her wicked broom.

At first, she wobbled from side to side and then fell around the broomstick with her head pointing towards the ground, only held to the stick with her feet wrapped tightly around each other.

But the weight of her long pointed nose and with the spiders jumping up and down her nose her legs broke free and she fell from the sky to the ground. Winnie B landed on a pile of fresh cow's dung, with a thud and splash.

Unharmed, she rose from the ground smelly and yelling, "I will get you another day! Mark my words, I will make you all pay!"

Broomie flew so fast, we were home in a jiffy, and just as we reached our home Eve & Jimmy were just arriving, that's our mum and dad.

Aunt Jean went home to her house, leaving us with a wink and a wave.

When our parents asked, "Did you have a great day?" We smiled, but did not let on!

Mum and Dad tucked us into our beds while Chippy and lassie cuddled into baby David, then all three rolled on their backs to get their bellies rubbed.

As Mum and Dad left the room, baby David spluttered out his first sentence, "Lock those windows and doors to keep out that bad witch."

Everyone laughed and shouted Goodnight! Sleep tight! Don't let those bedbugs bite, love you. Xxx

And those with well-trained ears could hear a faint echo beckoning from Winnie B's cottage... **Aha ha ha, I will get them back, mark my wicked words.**

Story Notes

Word Search: Find the Hidden word.
Hint: "Witches must xxxxx in themselves"

B E L I M E V W E K N N M E G
Z K M F C A I M E R T E M Q I
J K Y M L N G I N F K V F U L
K L K N N M M I A H C O M A I
M G K I F O H R C E A C R L A
B A E H O R C Y T T L M C I T
Y G R R C H E I J P B H W T Y
R D B G C T H E N P A N R Y X
P Z V T A W I V D N H S N M L
G N I L B T R W T O R P Q T N
Y W Q M T R N J K T M E L V H
P Z Q M K V P E T C K L T Y D
M M L O V E R M P B X L L T G
K R E D W G K T T Y F S R R M
Z W R A T L A X B E I N N I W

The word list

Ailig	Magic
Altar	Pentagram
Black	Red
Broomie	Spells
Chant	White
Coven	WinnieB
Equality	WinnieG
Freedom	Witch
Love	Witchcraft

My White Magic

Book of Shadows

Private Keep OUT!

This Spell Book belongs to:

____

My Book of Shadows

In this book of witchcraft,

I make my spells

Spells that tell

Do you smell them?

Can you?

Each potion that I create

Your senses they vacate

Until the magic is no mistake!

My spells are mine

And can only be cast by me

Nobody else will be able to cast my

spell...only me...Ahahaha.

Magic spells have been passed down by generations upon generations. In these pages of my book of shadows, I will write my spells, spells that I will create myself. I will use my imagination and research what is only good for me or good for others and add them to my spells. I will draw and write whatever I desire, for true and pure white magic is when one is free to write and draw with any creativity and without correction. Most of all, I will have loads of fun doing so. For I believe in myself.

Winnie G has given you two white magic spells (below) to begin your own book of shadows.

You are a good witch, your spells are only for good, and you will only cast good spells. If someone is being hurtful to you, then cast a good spell against their evil. And not against them. Remember, you will always be better than those that are evil towards you or others.

White magic is the purest form of magic that exists. It comes from the universe and rests in your heart. Use your magic to better yourself and the world around you. Live in freedom, peace and equality and you will grow to be the Good Witch.

Spell 1: To stop Nightmares

Spell 2: Getting rid of teenager spots or any spots on your face.

Bonus Spell 16: Requires a bit more effort and craft tools. But you can always put your guardians under a 'help me' spell.

Spells (Chants): Should always be said aloud, once.

The Witches Oath of Honour:

Take the witches oath before reading any further. You can say this oath once or whenever your believe wanders, but once said you live by it forever.

I'm a good witch

Past, present and future

My spells are cast

For good and protection

I love this universe

Everyone is one

We are all one

We live in peace, freedom and equality

No one that's good will come to harm with my spells.

I'm a good witch

The Witches Altar

Witches can have an altar, this is where you keep all your witchcraft items and cast your spells. You could have a Box as your portable altar, and keep all your magic tools inside. Or you could have a shelf in your room, where you place all your witchcraft items. Remember foods that can go off, should be stored in a fridge and discarded when due date has reached. All good witches make sure their health comes first and they do their magic in safety. Your witchcraft candles should never be left burning when no one is in the room, always have an adult present. You can always use Dream or LED Candles these do not have real flames, but will still carry the magic of the candle and are Winnie G witchcraft approved.

Candle Chant:

As the smoke rises, so does life's surprises

Your light, smell, touch and the air you breathe

Returns to the universe, For all that once was... Still is.

The starter Witchcraft altar/kit:

A box (To put all your witchcraft items in. Do not put your candle in this box, it must always stay free and in the open unless you are travelling. But first, make sure it has been extinguished for at least one hour☺ or better still use a Dream or LED Candle, they are safer and still have magic)

Pencils

Paper

Envelopes

Chocolate

Bananas

Imagination

A tablecloth (Or paper with a pentagram drawn on it and laid down to represent a small tablecloth)

Candle (Use safely, ask an adult or use a LED candle)

Magic Wand (Can be a piece of stick)

Pentagram (You can draw this on a piece of paper, there are some at the end of the Book, either tear out or make copies of the page. Better still make your own.)

Book of Shadows (That's this book)

Most of the items you can make yourself, that way you can save some money for a rainy day. There are items you can purchase if you want, but you don't have to do so to be a witch.

Before you Begin any Magic spells...

Use this chant to send Magic to all your Witchcraft tools, you only need do this once. Then all your tools will contain the magic. If you get new tools, then you must cast this chant to fill them with magic.

The magic Tool Chant

Said while holding or looking at the items. Remember, your tools of magic are your friends, they will be your magical assistants. You must say this chant to all new tools including food items that sit on your altar before they are used for the first time.

The Magic Tool Chant:

My Friends,

You cannot see

You cannot hear

You cannot smell

Everything on our earth can breathe, even stones can breath

You come from the universe

I ask you humbly to breathe my magic chant into your being

You are alive with magical powers

I thank you, my friends, for the power that you now provide me with

Witches never harm an animal or any other living creature to make spells no matter how small the creature is.

Witches cast spells from the goodness of their hearts to help others and themselves.

To the New Witch:

Spells sometimes do not work as you had planned. Don't worry it is not your fault! So why did my spell not work? Ok, everything that IS... Is part of the infinite universe. As such sometimes the universe will decide what magic it can allow. Sometimes the spell may not be in the best interest of everyone. Sometimes, we can get caught up in our own world, and what we want. But what we want sometimes is not enough, sometimes others that are involved need to want it as well. But always remember to cast your spells with your full believe and your best intentions, so don't worry if your spell did not work. You can always try again, sometimes a change to a spell will do a power of good. For example, you have spots, the spot spell did not work. But did you take care? Have you been washing your face regularly with unscented and pure soap?

Spells do not replace common sense. Spells work in conjunction with everything else that needs to be in place first. Spells give you the power to believe in yourself. Before you can love another, you must love yourself. Spells cannot force another to do what you want, but they can help you achieve what is good for you. And if the universe wishes it to be the same... then it will be so.

Spells are cast to help others, and that includes our natural world. Witches never harm animals or our natural environment. A witch never uses the blood of anything for their spells. A true Witch is at one with themselves and the universe around us all.

Create your spells and cast them well. But remember have loads of fun, and always enjoy what you do. And only create good spells.

Spell ideas can come from research.

Research what is good for you and the universe.

You can read books, online and by sitting quietly in a room.

Five minutes of meditation per day will help your imagination go a long way.

You have 13 spells that you can create yourself in your book of shadows plus the three that Winnie G gave you, that's 16 spells of witchcraft. Think what you want your spell to do. Help someone? Empower yourself? Find happiness? And many of the other ideas that come into your imagination. There is no hurry to create spells, take your time and enjoy.

The book of shadows is your personal journey, your personal thoughts, it's your diary of your life. Its pages will eventually contain your feelings, happiness, sadness, sweat, aspirations, hopes and pain. This book is your roadmap throughout your life's journey, so enjoy.

The five elements:

Fire

Earth

Air

Water

Yourself. You are the lifeform element.

These five elements are the energies that surround us and are part of your witchcraft. The elements are part of your universe.

The pentagram represents the five elements.

The circle that you will draw on the ground around you. (Or you can place a pentagram on the ground around where you will cast your spells. If there is more than one witch, then each of you will stand within the circle of pentagram's that you place on the floor around you.)

The circle helps to contain your witchcraft, the magic energy and to keep evil forces at bay.

Your pentagram points north, west, east and south (South has 2 points, this is represented by SOUTH and YOU. (See the Witches Pentagram below.) The True south point as per a compass is the middle point between 'south' and 'you' pointing in the opposite direction from north.

Each point represents an element. Sometimes witches use the following colours of a candle to represent the elements. Candles can be placed on your floor to represent this. (Only use Led dream or led candles – do not use 'lit' candles. Lit candles should be used with care and with an adult present)

North (Earth) (Green Candle)
South (Fire) (Red Candle)
West (Water) (Blue Candle)
East (Air) (Yellow Candle)

The Fifth Element (YOU): You are the spiritual energy. Your colour is that of a rainbow and your shape is that of a star. You are 'one' with the universe and the universe is 'one' with all that exists.

The Witches pentagram

A witch's health:

Witches look after their health when doing their witchcraft by:

Wash your hands before and after handling food

When using food items for consumption, make sure you store it correctly

Never eat any food items that are 'off' or past the due by date

Never eat food items that you are allergic to. Example. If you are allergic to chocolate then you must not eat it or use it. In these instances, you will replace the spell ingredients by using another item that is OK for you to eat or be near.

Candles, I recommend Dream or LED candles, these do not require to be lit, and they still contain all the magic of other types of candles. However, if you are using candles that you light with a flame, then you must make sure, that an adult supervises you.

Never be alone with any open flames. Keep all your witchcraft items away from young children or anything that is flammable.

Keep all of your witchcraft items together either in your witchcraft box or your altar.

Notes:

Notes:

Notes:

About Witchcraft Kits

If you are **a teenager** you can use LED candles or candles that you can light (of course it may still be subject to a responsible adults consent?)

If you are **not a teenager,** then you should definitely use a LED candle, they are safer and less Messy. And your witchcraft will be just as great.

The Witchcraft kit that you will need is sorted in order of what you require for spell 1 and 2. The other items will help you make further spells. As your ideas and spells grow so will the tools that you will require.

1 - Magic Wand (can be any piece of stick)

2 - Chalk for making your circle

3 - Pencil

4 - White pentagram paper (you can use plain paper and draw your own pentagram on it – Your book of shadows contains 10 pieces of pentagram paper that you can gently tear or cut from this book and use for your spells)

5 - Chocolate bar (dark or milk)

6 - Candle (preferably a LED candle. IMPORTANT: If you use a candle that needs to be lit, then you must ensure a responsible adult is with you at all times!)

7 - Banana (s)

8 - **Book of Shadows** (That's this book)

9 - **Pentagram altar cloth** (Or one piece of pentagram paper laid down to represent a cloth. It does not matter if it only covers a small area of the table. You can invest in a cloth at a later time if you want)

10 - **Imagination, lots of it**

11 - **Box or altar, to put all your witchcraft items in.** [Altar can be a shelf or table in your room. Never put a hot candle into a box or cupboard. Your box can be plain or you can decorate it with anything that your heart desires.]

All of the above is for Spell 1 and 2. The items below are for the bonus spell.

12 – (4 x Herbs) Introduction (Get from any supermarket)

Fennell (**Good for** aiding digestions. **Use to** keep curses away. **How to use**, eat a tiny bit raw, or mix in with any potion. It tastes a little like liquorice before and after casting your spell)

Garlic (**Good for** digestion, hair and skin. **Use for** magical healing for your inner body. **How to use**, eat a tiny amount before and after you cast your spell. You can mix it in your potions as well. Don't rub your eyes after use...they will sting)

Ginger (**Good for** travel sickness or any sickness. **Use for** relaxation or after a large meal. **How to use**, each a tiny bit before and after casting your spell or mix it with a potion)

Jasmine (**Good for** nerves. **Use for** attracting Love or money. **How to use** make a small drink with it and sip before and after casting your spell)

13 - A pentagram pendant (optional)

14 - Essential Oil [not for eating]

15 - 3 Crystals (Optional)

16 - Unscented Potpourri or it can be a mixture of flowers, leafs and petals [not for eating]

17 - Mixing Bowl

Notes

Notes:

Where to purchase your witchcraft items:

Some Witchcraft items can be purchased at Winnie G's witchcraft shop. Or you can buy them at any other store. Some items you may have in your home already. Some items you can create and make yourself. You don't need to spend a lot of money on your witchcraft supplies. Make do with what you have.

Notes:

Spell 1:

<u>To Stop Nightmare's</u>

Are you having nightmares? Then the nightmare spell will remove or reduce their power over you. Letting you sleep with ease and being at one with your dreams.

<u>Tools needed:</u>

Pencil (not pen)

Paper (white)

An envelope (colour and size do not matter) If you don't have an envelope fold it inside another piece of paper.

Chocolate (dark or milk)

The Magic spell (The Chant)

The Spell (Chant once)

Happy face, I desire

Sad face, covered in chocolate

Scary face covered in chocolate

Sad and Scary face is no longer my nightmare

Happy face is my desire

I cast this spell, and my nightmares shall no longer scare me

What to do:

1 - On the piece of paper, draw a happy face and immediately next to it draw a sad face. Underneath both faces draw a scary face.

2 - Get your chocolate and lick your finger, rub your wet finger on the

chocolate until you have some chocolate melted onto your finger.

3 - Rub your chocolate finger on the sad and scary face.

4 - While holding the paper in your hand. (You must look at the paper while saying your spell. Now! Cast your spell, you must do it with belief

5 - Fold the paper up and place it into the envelope

6 - Place the envelope under your pillow before you go to sleep.

If your nightmares return in the future, repeat all of your steps and cast your spell again.

My personal Notes to the Spell 1:

Spell 2:

Get rid of spots

Are you fed up with spots, or acne as it is called? Well, these are a natural occurrence as your body changes. No spell can remove these, for to do so, would mean having to change the future evolution of everyone on earth.

But... casting a spell will help make them disappear and carry on their work hidden from prying faces. But remember all witches should eat healthily. You must believe in what you are doing or the magic will not work.

Tools Required:

Piece of white paper

Pencil (not pen)

A small banana still in its skin (or half a large banana – keep the other half for tomorrow night's spell)

An envelope (colour and size do not matter) If you don't have an envelope fold it inside another piece of paper.

The Magic Spell (Chant Once)

The Spell (Chant Once)

My face! My face!

What has my youth done to me?

Spots are good to me

My spots I love

My spots will heal

I cast this spell on my spots to bother me no more

<u>**What to do**</u>

1   - Do these steps at least 1 hour before you go to bed for your night's rest.

2   - Take the paper and draw two faces on it

3   - On one of the faces draw as many spots as you think you have

4   - On the other face, draw a happy face with two small spots.

5   - Now, peel the banana and eat all of the banana.

6   - Take one piece of the banana skin and rub it on the paper face with all the spots that you pencilled.

7   - Take the remaining banana skin and rub the inside of the skin onto the spots on your own face. Rub

it all over every spot that you have.

8 - Now, take your spell and chant with belief and meaning 3 times.

10 - Fold the paper with the faces and position into the envelope. Just before you go to bed place the envelope under your pillow.

11 - Do this every night for the first week. Then at least twice a week thereafter or until your happy.

Remember your spots may fade or they may remain. If they remain, continue to rub a fresh banana skin on those pesky spots and eat ½ a banana daily (remembering to say your chant.) If they still remain, then they are not ready to

leave you yet. But you are ready to love
and accept them.

My personal Notes to the Spell 2:

Spell 3:

Spell 4:

Spell 5:

Spell 6:

Spell 7:

Spell 8:

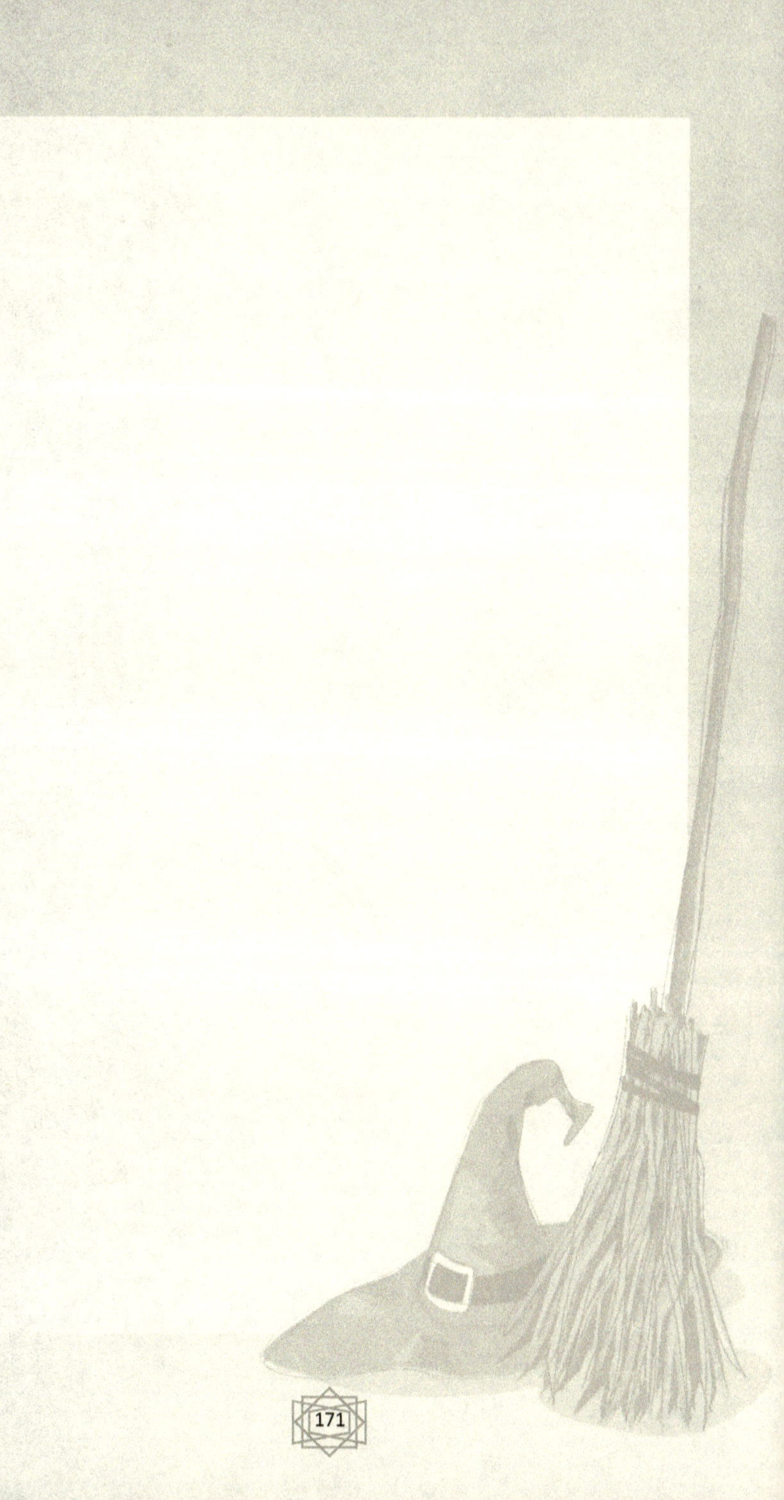

Spell 9:

Spell 10:

Spell 11:

Spell 12:

There is no spell 13, that's because the 13th spell is reserved for the highest of the witches, Winnie G. She is the only one that can cast a 13th spell, without it turning into Bad Magic. Bad magic is what Winnie B uses. JUST DON'T DO IT!

Spell 14:

Spell 15:

BONUS Spell 16
<u>To lift Sadness</u>

Just for you my male and female witches!

This is a quick spell for when you feel sad. And we witches are like anyone else we can get sad too!

You can use this to cast a spell to help your family, friends and yourself.

You will need:

A few drops of 'Ylang Ylang' Essential Oil, a bag of Potpourri (a bowl full), a **Lepidolite**

Chrystal, a **mixing bowl** and a **bowl** to put your potion mixture into.

How to: Put your potpourri into the mixing bowl, then add the crystal, then add 5 drops of essential oils. Mix it all together with your hands while saying your spell. Once mixed and spell said, take out the Chrystal and hold it in your hand. Clean the Chrystal and put it back on your altar or box. Rub your hands together, so you are rubbing the oil into your skin.

The Spell (Chant)

With this spell I cast

The air is stale
I don't want my spell to fail
We are sad
Yet we are far from bad

The air we now breathe is fresh
This new aroma surrounds our flesh

Sadness is one of our emotions that reside in our hearts
But for a while, I need you to DEPART
Please leave sadness
So we can be filled with happiness

What you need to do: To cast the sadness spell: Always remember to have done the new tool chant (if you have not already done so)

1 - Put your pentagram paper down on the table or altar.

2 - Mix your ingredients and Chrystal [remember to say your spell as you mix]

3 - Take out the Chrystal (Lepidolite**), hold it in your hand. Next, clean the Chrystal with your hands and put back on your altar. Your hands will now be filled with the magic potion.

4 - Take the bowl and leave it in the room where everyone visits. Say your spell in every room your bowl stands.

5 - Remember to speak in a positive manner when talking to anyone in that room. Because negative thoughts and talks will undo all that magic you have just created.

6 - In a day or two, and when the sweet aroma stops smelling, you can add a few drops of essential oil to the bowl, while saying you Sadness Spell. This will help your spell last a wee bit longer.

** If you do not have a Lepidolite Chrystal, use another Chrystal and charge it with your tool chant.

Spell 16 Notes:

5 pages for Notes, Drawings and Ideas

It's not the end, it's only the beginning. Ahahaha

North
West
East
Towards South
South
You

North
West
East
Towards South
South
You

North
West
East
Towards South
South
You

North
West
East
Towards South
South
You

North
West
East
Towards South
South
You

North
West
East
Towards South
South
You

North
West
East
Towards South
South
You

North
West
East
Towards South
South
You

North
West
East
Towards South
South
You

North
West
East
Towards South
South
You

228

North
West
East
Towards South
South
You

BE AWARE of...

Please note: Witchcraft and witches are a part of the fabric of our superstitions created throughout our history on earth.

This book is a fun youth's book, but it would not hurt an adult to practice the same rituals within.

What this book is not: This book is not a historical fact! Nor may it fully resemble other books of witchcraft.

This book is Winnie G's witchcraft.

The book does: Contain some known and documented items of original witchcraft. But the main theme is for the youth to have fun and in a safe environment.

Do not:

Participate in anything with people you do not know, regardless of the similarities or sympathy's that they may have or share with what you do. **And** always check with a responsible adult, even when not in any doubt. Because evil people go on holidays too!

Notes

Notes

Notes

Word Search: Find the Hidden Word'
Hint: "A witch will xxx the ingredients together"

```
M  I  L  L  A  X  S  R  N  G  N  T
X  P  K  K  G  P  S  I  H  T  V  C
H  A  V  E  E  R  K  T  X  A  B  G
W  N  L  L  V  R  H  D  O  H  Y  W
Y  W  L  N  Q  V  X  L  R  W  U  D
Y  R  E  V  E  A  L  S  H  O  D  O
M  E  W  Y  T  H  H  Y  Y  Z  M  O
A  J  H  M  C  L  X  M  O  W  D  G
G  K  V  T  V  M  J  K  I  U  C  D
I  R  I  R  S  R  D  T  X  R  R  D
C  W  Q  W  M  I  H  L  D  R  X  O
V  S  T  N  E  I  D  E  R  G  N  I
```

Word List

all	the
do	this
Good	to
have	what
ingredients	Witch
is	with
magic	you
Reveals	your
spell	

Register at:

https://www.jeanmegaw.com

To be kept up-to-date with her new releases and to become a registered Winnie G Witch.

Thank you for purchasing my book

Thanks To:
Izakowski, vgorbash, Ptkang and
prometeus
For providing the Photo Art.
Font by Blambot Comics

North
West
East
Towards South
South
You